WHISPER™
THE WINGED UNICORN

Curse of the Dragon

Written by Christopher Brown
Illustrated by Tom Kinarney
Reading Level Consultant: JoAnn Mahle, M.A., Ed.

 Antioch Publishing Company
Yellow Springs, Ohio 45387

Copyright © 1985 Antioch Publishing Company
Made in the United States of America
ISBN 0-89954-401-0

Whisper was grazing in the upper meadows of Rainbow Forest. She liked to come here on warm afternoons. It was so quiet and peaceful, a place where she could relax and daydream undisturbed. Although she loved the other creatures in the forest, they had a way of taking all her time. "Whisper, can you help me with this?" "Whisper, what do you think about that?" Unicorns were wise and magical—all the legends said so. A unicorn's advice was worth seeking, but sometimes Whisper wished that her friends didn't seek it so often! It was good to feel needed, good to be helpful. But even a unicorn needed time alone. Whisper came to the meadows just to get away, to think things out. Afterward she could return to her friends with a fresh outlook.

Whisper stretched, shivering from nose to tail. What a wonderful day to be alive! The grass was crisp and sweet as it always was in mid-summer. Nearby, a cool brook sang invitingly. Not a cloud marred the deep blue sky. After lunch she planned to find a shady spot and treat herself to a nap. Everyone deserved a lazy afternoon once in a while.

She ambled over to the brook to quench her thirst. A frog jumped with a splash. In the slower water, minnows wagged their tails against the current. A lazy afternoon indeed!

Suddenly from across the meadow came a squeaking cry. "Whisper! Whisper, where are you?" Raising her wet muzzle, Whisper turned toward the sound. She saw only waving tufts of grass. "Whisper!"

the cry came again, closer this time. Long ears and a white cotton tail turned this way and that. Bixby the Rabbit!

"Over here!" called Whisper.

On a nearby hillock, the little rabbit popped out of the grass. His nose twitched. He looked worried. Catching sight of Whisper, he ducked again, scurrying toward the brook.

"Whisper, you've got to come," Bixby panted, his hind paw thumping the ground. "It's D-D-Dorian! S-Something's wrong."

Whisper felt a chill of fear. "What do you mean, something's wrong?"

"Dorian's down in Squishmire Marsh in the old part of the forest," stammered Bixby, his paw still thumping. "He's covered with sp-sp-spots!"

"What!"

"Yes, and h-he says…he says he's *sick* and everyone p-please leave him alone."

"Dorian's never been sick a day in his life," said Whisper. She knew how Bixby tended to exaggerate. But as she looked at his little pinched face, she felt sure he was telling the truth. The fear inside her grew. "I'd better see for myself!"

Leaving Bixby to fret alone, Whisper spread her wings and soared upward. Beneath her the broad meadowland shrank to patches of yellow and green.

To the eastward, Rainbow Forest stretched mile after shadowy mile. But to Whisper the enchantment of the forest was dimmed. Somewhere down there Dorian the Dragon, her oldest and dearest friend, was in trouble!

Squishmire Marsh was a chain of ponds where strange plants grew and stranger creatures lived. Lilies floated in pools. Moss hung thickly in the ancient trees, making them look like hairy trolls. Vines, creepers, and soggy ground discouraged intruders. No one in Rainbow Forest knew much about the marsh, and none of the marsh creatures ever came out for a visit.

Spiraling down, Whisper began to search for Dorian. She skimmed the surface of the ponds, the wind from her wings ruffling the water as she passed. Silence hung over the marsh. Whisper sensed suspicious eyes following her. Once she heard scurrying in the brambles on shore as some shy creature sped away.

Deep in the marsh, she finally saw her friend. Dorian lay in the mud near shore. His colors looked faded. His scales were covered with ugly green spots.

On the bank a small group of Rainbow Forest residents were doing their best to help. "It's about time you got here!" exclaimed crabby Grandmother Bear as

Whisper landed. "I hope you know how to make sense to this stubborn dragon. I surely can't!"

Dorian raised his eyes to Whisper and tried to smile. "It's dragon bane," he said, his voice weak. "There must be some growing nearby. It was foolish of me to drink this water."

"Dragon bane?" asked Whisper. "What's that?"

"It's a rare herb. In ancient times the wizards used it to bend dragons to evil purposes. I'm afraid I've swallowed quite a dose."

Dorian breathed a tired sigh. He rested his scaly chin on a log and blinked back tears. "In fact, my friends, this is the end of me."

"What!" cried Whisper.

Grandmother Bear spoke up. "That's what he's been saying for hours, 'the end of me, the end of me.' He won't say any more."

"Do you mean," asked Whisper, terror in her voice, "that you're going to die?"

Dorian sighed again. "No, I'm not going to die," he answered. "I'm going to *change*." The way he said "change" made Whisper shudder.

"The wizards used dragon bane to create the great monsters of the legends," said Dorian. "Normally dragons are gentle, loving creatures. But a potion made from dragon bane can change them into horrid beasts of destruction. That's what the bane in this marsh water is doing to me."

"NO!"

Again, Dorian tried to smile. "Yes, my dear Whisper. I *know* the truth. You and everyone else in Rainbow Forest will be in grave danger unless you destroy me before the fire grows."

The little group at the edge of the marsh stood in shocked silence. Finally Whisper said, "I don't believe it. You must be mistaken."

"I'm sorry to say I'm not," said Dorian. "Stories of dragon bane fill our history. But it seems so long ago now. I never thought...I never thought that in Squishmire Marsh, of all places, I'd find it growing." Dorian raised his head, a pleading look on his face. "You must protect yourselves," he insisted. "If you destroy me now, I won't fight you. I'll be grateful. But later...Oh, Whisper, you've never seen an evil dragon. With dragon bane controlling me, I could wipe out all of Rainbow Forest."

"NEVER!" exclaimed Whisper, still disbelieving. "There must be another way."

"Sometimes, Whisper, we are called upon to do unpleasant tasks for the sake of others. To rid me of this evil would be a kindness, and to save Rainbow Forest is your duty. You have no choice."

Dorian's friends were weeping openly. Even Grandmother Bear cluck, cluck, clucked and shook her head. Only Whisper, whose friendship with Dorian spanned her whole life, felt something else. She felt anger! Her eyes blazed out.

"I won't allow it!" she cried. "Nothing could make me hurt you!"

"Whisper…" Dorian began gently.

"NO!"

Turning to the others, Whisper said, "Stay with him. Try to bring him whatever he needs, but DO NOT listen to what he says. I'll be back soon."

Whisper launched herself from the bank and streaked out of the marsh. Dorian's parting words rang in her ears: "You're wasting your time!"

Indeed, as she circled over Rainbow Forest, Whisper felt that she *was* wasting her time. Try as she might, she could think of nothing that would save Dorian. She floated gracefully on the warm air, but flight was joyless. The sun warmed the backs of her wings, but she hardly noticed. Passing birds took one look at Whisper's miserable face and wisely stayed away.

Far below, Laughing River cut through the forest. Ahead, the mighty waterfall—forest creatures called it Old Roarer—sent up clouds of steam.

Steam! Whisper remembered something. Long ago she had visited a place hidden in fogs and steams, a place of legend and mystery. Dark Hollow! There she

had met Phineas. The Morg, he called himself, which meant historian. "We helped protect this country during the troll invasions," he had said. "The trolls were driven away, but my people were also scattered. Only I remain."

Phineas kept a library full of the knowledge of his people. Maybe he knew about ancient wizards. Maybe he knew a cure for dragon bane. If anyone could help Dorian, it would be Phineas the Morg!

Brimming with new hope, Whisper flew off toward Dark Hollow.

"Well, Whisper!" said Phineas from the entrance to his cave. "What a delight! I haven't seen you in a long while. Come in, come in!"

He was just as she remembered him, short, bald, and wrinkled. His eyes looked huge behind his spectacles, but they were friendly. His cave was as she remembered it too. If anything, it was more cluttered than ever with books and scrolls. "One always fears what one doesn't understand," he had once told her. "My library is my key to understanding. Through books, I hear voices of the past. Their wisdom guides me toward the future."

"Phineas, something terrible has happened!"

"Yes, yes, I thought so. You seem anxious." Phineas removed his spectacles, blew on them, then wiped them on the hem of his robe. "How may I help you?" he asked, sitting on a toadstool.

When Whisper finished her story, Phineas rubbed his chin. "Hmmmm, yes, yes," he said. "I've heard of dragon bane. Dorian is right. Those old-time dragons were terrible to behold! Fire-breathers, they were, with claws fit to tear a hillside down."

From a stack in one corner, Phineas withdrew a yellow scroll. He blew dust from it and examined its ragged edges. "Mice!" he said. "Always nibbling my books. That's what you call 'digesting information.' Ha! Ha!"

Unrolling the scroll, he began to read, mumbling, *"History of Wizards, Warlocks, and Witches,* compiled

by Phineas Morganus—that's me! Let's see now...
daggers...demons...dragon...dragon bane!"

Phineas sat down and for some time was absorbed in the scroll. As she waited, Whisper tried to restrain her impatience. She swished her tail, she stretched her wings, she scuffed her hooves on the hard cave floor. At last, Phineas looked up.

"Bad news," he said. "The effects of dragon bane can't be reversed. Wizards knew how, but they guarded their secret well. Alas, Whisper, no wizard remains to tell us. Their knowledge is lost. Dorian is right, my dear. We cannot allow a Fire-breather in Rainbow Forest. All of us would perish."

"Can't you do anything?" demanded Whisper.

Again Phineas rubbed his chin. "Perhaps I could slow things down a little. Let me see...somewhere I have information on the care and feeding of friendly dragons. If I could hold off the dragon bane, you might have time."

"Time for what?" Whisper exclaimed.

"Why, time to find Wizards' Roost, of course. I'm not sure where it is—the old rumors aren't clear. I've always meant to search it out, thinking I might find information for my book. Never quite had time—you know how it is."

"But what's Wizards' Roost?" asked Whisper.

"The Roost was the source of evil power in the old days. War, disease, hunger, all the ugliness in the world, arose from that dreadful place. My people paid a terrible price to destroy it. Now Dorian's only hope lies in your finding it again, finding some way to stop the curse of dragon's bane. Are you willing?"

"YES!" cried Whisper eagerly.

Rainbow Forest lay far behind. Ahead waited gray mountain crags. Dark clouds hid the sun. Cold air streamed around Whisper's wings. Already she was frightened. Eerie tales of wizards, trolls, and long-ago battles were fine when you heard them at home among friends. But now, as she flew toward lands of legend that no one had seen for a thousand years, she felt the presence of ghosts. Horrible events had stained the evil realm forever.

"Fly north until you find the Mountain of Fire," Phineas had said. "That's all I know. My books tell no more. Wizards' Roost is nearby. Good luck!"

Mountain of Fire, thought Whisper. What did that mean? As cold as it was growing, fire would be welcome. Even a mountain of it! She flew hard against the wind just to keep warm.

Snow fell from the gray clouds. Whisper flew lower, skimming rocky peaks. Dim valleys opened before her, then even higher peaks. Her wings ached. She longed for a rest. But Phineas had warned her, "Waste not a moment. I don't know how long I can postpone the change in Dorian. Hurry, my dear!"

Then she saw it, a mountain faintly red against the clouds in the distance. The red glow flickered, went out, flickered again. As she flew closer, the glow became a glare. A huge, cone-shaped mountain rose above its neighbors, and from its summit shot sparks and tongues of flame. Smoke blended with the clouds. The air grew thick. She had found it! The Mountain of Fire!

She could hear the mountain's thunder, could feel it crashing against her in waves of heat. The mountain seemed angered by her intrusion. Whisper's eyes were dazzled by the brightness. The light pulled at her as though she were a moth. Closer and closer! Her ears rang with the mountain's roar. The heat...the heat...

Just before she fainted, Whisper sensed that she was falling.

Phineas the Morg sat on the bank of Squishmire Marsh. He was eating a raspberry tart that Grandmother Bear had baked for him. Since he rarely left his cave in Dark Hollow, everyone treated him as an honored visitor. Phineas was pleased.

"This is delicious," he said to Dorian. "When you're well again, Grandmother Bear will bake you a basketful."

Dorian scowled. His green spots had become blotches, and his tongue flicked out like that of an angry snake. The dragon bane was advancing.

"Home remedies aren't the best," Phineas confessed casually. "Nasty-tasting, I'm sure. But that's as it should be. Tomorrow we'll give you a little stronger dose, a bucketful. That is, if that young rascal Bixby can find more wild butterbalm for the mixture. How do you feel?"

A hissing sigh escaped the dragon's lips. "It's getting worse," he growled. "I'm losing control of myself, Phineas."

The Morg shook his raspberry tart. "Have courage, old friend. You'll get through this. The beavers are out cutting strong vines. We'll tie you down if we need to." Phineas grinned. "I learned a few good knots when I was a lad."

It was very cold. Whisper shivered and shook her head. She was sprawled in a bank of snow. Above her loomed the black cone of the Mountain of Fire. The roaring had stopped. Only a faint pink glow still lit the clouds.

"My, my," she muttered to herself. Her silky wings were singed. She felt sore, as though she'd tumbled down the mountainside. Maybe she had! She couldn't remember.

Suddenly Whisper heard the snow crunching behind her. Whirling, she saw something that made her squeak with alarm. Another unicorn! The biggest, blackest, most beautiful unicorn she had ever seen. He stamped a foreleg in the snow and stared with ice-cold eyes. As he tossed his magnificent head, steam billowed from his nostrils.

"Hello," said Whisper meekly. She thought of how silly she looked after her encounter with the mountain. "I think I'm lost."

With royal dignity, the strange unicorn approached. He stood head and shoulders above her and seemed too proud to speak.

Whisper introduced herself. "I'm Whisper the Winged Unicorn," she said. "I live in Rainbow Forest."

"Then you are lost indeed."

"I'm looking for Wizards' Roost," said Whisper.

The black unicorn lifted his head and the peaks echoed his laughter. "You have journeyed for nothing, little friend. I am Falco, lord of this region. Wizards' Roost was dust a thousand years before you were born. All that remains is that grotto yonder. I've made

it my home. Come, you need rest and sweet grass before your return trip."

Whisper hung her head. "I came on an important mission," she said sadly. "A friend is depending on me."

"Come!" said Falco. "We'll talk of it later. First, food and rest."

Without hope, Whisper followed Falco's broad hoofprints through the snow.

Falco's grotto had been carved from black rock which perfectly matched his coat. Its high ceiling glowed as though someone had polished it. Deep inside, a huge stone trough brimmed with cool water, and nearby stood bin after bin of grain and tender grass.

"What is this mission of which you speak?" Falco asked as Whisper refreshed herself.

She explained Dorian's plight, Falco listening with keen interest.

"Dragon bane, yes. I've heard the tales. Have you no unicorn magic with which to defeat him?"

Whisper bowed her head. "What magic I have is of no use. I'm too young and inexperienced. Besides, those of us in Rainbow Forest have no wish to defeat him. We only want to help."

Falco stared long and hard with his icy eyes. "Why do you love this dragon so much?" he asked.

"Dorian is huge and fierce-looking," said Whisper. "No other creature could overpower him. Yet he chooses to be gentle. He goes his own way, troubling no one, helping all those in need. He has watched over me since I was very young. I've learned from him that the greatest power isn't strength, but love of others. For love of those in Rainbow Forest, he asked us to destroy him."

"And for love of him you've undertaken this quest," said Falco. "Perhaps I can help you."

Whisper stared, eyes wide, mouth open. "*Could you?* Oh, how can I ever thank you?"

Smiling, Falco said, "By showing me this wonderful beast Dorian. I'm very curious to see a dragon. I know many things about the old wizards, including the secret of dragon bane. Rest now, little friend. Soon we'll return to your Rainbow Forest."

Whisper resented the need to rest. Time was so important to Dorian. But she was too tired to go on. Curling up on a soft bed of straw, she composed herself to sleep. A shadow passed over her. Whisper opened her eyes. Muttering strange words under his breath, Falco was staring into the mirrored surface of a large stone. Whisper could see his reflection. The face was Falco's, yet different too. In the shiny stone, the beautiful black unicorn looked very much like an ugly, bearded wizard!

Poor Dorian felt like a fly
tangled in spiderwebs. Thick
vines crisscrossed his body.
Phineas had supervised tying
him down, deeming his comfort
less important than preventing his
escape. The vines were fastened to
stakes driven deep in the ground.
Dorian would have to
struggle hard before
he got away.

"Three buckets of medicine today," said Phineas to Bixby. "By tomorrow, he'll be too wild to let us give it to him."

"W-what's keeping Wh-Whisper?" stammered Bixby, peeking around Phineas' robe. The change in Dorian was by now too terrifying for the little rabbit. He couldn't bear to see. Phineas himself looked old and tired. He had stayed awake all night tending the ailing dragon and it was beginning to show.

"Patience," advised the Morg, scratching Bixby's ears. "I have faith in that young unicorn. If anyone can save Dorian, she can. Come, let's gather more butterbalm."

As they hurried away, a low hissing filled the dreary marsh. Dorian's yellow eyes glared menacingly. He raised his head, but the vines still held fast. Angrily, he hissed again. From the corner of his mouth, a thread of smoke began to rise.

"S-s-s-so…you've made me a prisoner," he snarled. "Well, soon you'll pay, all of you. S-s-s-soon!"

Falco turned back from the shiny stone. His face was normal again, the same beautiful unicorn that Whisper had first admired. But the memory of the ugly reflection troubled her. From her pile of straw, Whisper watched Falco through half-closed eyes. Something was wrong—she felt uneasy, as though some evil presence filled the grotto. She stirred in the straw and Falco looked her way.

"Troubled sleep?" he asked. "Perhaps a soothing drink of herb tea would help."

"No, thank you," said Whisper. Her suspicions were growing. Rising to her feet, she said, "Who are you?"

Falco eyed her haughtily. "As I told you, I am Falco, lord of these mountains. Here, no wind blows, no snow falls, without my permission. I command all!"

"Including the Mountain of Fire?" asked Whisper. "I felt the pull of the mountain. It was drawing me. Did you command it to do so?"

Falco nodded, showing his fine white teeth.

"You are no unicorn!" cried Whisper, backing up. "No unicorn works evil. You're a wizard, aren't you?"

Falco's smile became even brighter. Whisper blinked as the image of the black unicorn began to change. It seemed to melt, to waver like air on a hot day, to reshape itself. Whisper shook her head, and when she looked again, she saw not a black unicorn but the ugly, bearded wizard from the stone!

"What do you want from me?" Whisper demanded.

The wizard laughed harshly. "Why, your dragon friend, of course! With Dorian under my power, I will be able to restore Wizards' Roost to its former glory. I have waited—oh, how I've waited—for a chance like this. Three ingredients were all I needed: dragon bane, a dragon, and...YOU!"

"ME!" Whisper exclaimed.

The wizard spread his withered hands. "Of course," he said. "There is but one way to control the effects of dragon bane. The old spellbinders searched for centuries until they found it. Balance the evil effects of dragon bane with something pure and innocent, some substance rare and unspoiled. Too little and the monster is uncontrollable. Too much and the dragon becomes good again. You need just the right mixture of good and evil to create a useful Firebreather. And what is this magic substance, you ask?" The wizard laughed again, horribly. "That substance, my four-legged friend, is unicorn horn!"

Whisper gasped. The shadows of the grotto seemed to ensnare her. She backed up more.

"What is rarer than a unicorn?" the wizard continued. "Today when your image appeared in my magic stone, I was overjoyed! Not only a unicorn, mind you, but one who can fly! I searched endlessly for what, in the end, came searching for me."

"So not all the wizards were destroyed in the old wars," said Whisper.

"All save one. Me! Falco the Great! And soon I shall have my revenge. Your horn is the key!"

Falco stretched forth his hand. Whisper shrank away. She remembered his words: *too much unicorn horn and an evil dragon turned good again.* With that secret, she could save Dorian. Never, never, would the wizard lay hands on her horn. Anger rose in Whisper. "STAY BACK!" she warned.

Suddenly a bright yellow bolt shot from Whisper's horn. Falco howled in pain. Shaking his scorched fingers, the wizard danced around the grotto. "I might have guessed, I might have guessed!" he whined.

Whisper was just as surprised as Falco. Such power was new to her.

"The Force of Good!" cried Falco. "It protects you. While you live I can't touch the horn!" The wizard pointed a shaking finger. "We'll soon take care of that! Sealed in this grotto, you will not last long," cackled Falco. "Then the horn will be mine!"

He rushed out. From the entrance came the rumble of falling rocks. Falco's magic had brought down an avalanche! The grotto filled with darkness. Whisper was trapped!

Lying on the straw, Whisper wept in despair. She had failed Dorian. Gladly would she give her horn, even her life, to save her friend. How foolish she had been not to see through Falco's trickery. Now both she and Dorian were doomed.

From the back of the grotto came the slow *drip, drip, drip* of seeping water. Each drop marked a moment lost. Rising, Whisper felt her way toward the sound. Something drew her. Something inside herself said, "Don't give up. Your magic, too, is strong."

As she went step by step, she noticed a change. The blackness of the grotto was slowly turning to gray. With each step the grayness brightened. At last Whisper found herself in a huge cavern. A small hole high overhead admitted daylight. Waves of joy swept over her. Escape! Falco had made a mistake. In sealing the cave, he had forgotten the one thing that made Whisper different from other unicorns. She could fly!

Taking careful aim, she shot up, up and through the narrow opening. The daylight was blinding. Cliffs and giant boulders surrounded her. She weaved and dodged, banking left and right. Suddenly the obstacles fell away. A valley stretched out below. Beyond it rose the smoking Mountain of Fire. As she streaked past, it hardly rumbled at all. Safe! She was safe!

In the south the sky was clear. Whisper flew like an arrow. Home, home to Rainbow Forest. Home to Dorian.

On a hill overlooking Squishmire Marsh stood Phineas, Bixby, Grandmother Bear, and the Beaver family. They feared to approach closer. Dorian had already torn most of the vines to bits. A few more and he would be free! The marsh echoed with his roars. Vivid blasts of flame curled from his mouth. Gentle, loving Dorian was gone.

"I-i-isn't there anything we c-c-can do?" asked Bixby for the hundredth time.

Phineas picked him up, stroking his soft fur. "All that's left is for us to flee," the Morg said grimly. "I've sent messengers through the forest. Everyone is packing. My ancestors had ways of fighting Fire-breathers, but I have none."

With a whiplike snap, another vine broke. Dorian stretched his neck and roared, setting the air ablaze.

"Time to get the young'uns out of here," said Papa Beaver. "Shoo, you kids! Make for the river." Three little flat tails scampered into the bushes. "So long, friends," Papa called as he and Mama departed as well.

"I guess we'd better go too," said Phineas. "It's too painful to remain."

Just then, Grandmother Bear pointed upward. "My stars! What's that?"

The group on the hill squinted into the distance. A streak of white was rocketing toward Squishmire Marsh.

"It's Whisper!" cried Bixby. "I know it is!"

Sure enough, not a moment later, Whisper circled the marsh. She looked gray and weather-beaten as she fluttered down to the hilltop, but her eyes sparkled with excitement.

"I've found it! I've found the cure!" The others rushed to her side. "It's my horn," Whisper continued. "Phineas, make a powder out of my horn and give it to Dorian. Quickly!"

Phineas brushed aside Whisper's forelock. "I'm sorry, my dear. It's too late. I couldn't get close enough to Dorian now to give him anything. Look at him."

For the first time, Whisper viewed the raging inferno that had once been her friend. She gasped. Tears sprang to her eyes.

"I won't give up! Not now! Please, Phineas, do as I ask. I'll make him take it somehow."

Another vine snapped. Dorian reared up, roaring, pawing the air. Bixby squeaked and hid in the folds of Phineas' robe.

"Very well," the Morg said. "Let's try." He scratched his head. "Ah!" Reaching into his knapsack, Phineas produced a small stone flask. "Butterbalm drippings," he explained. Then, from his pocket, he withdrew a small silver knife. "Now hold still, my dear." Whisper braced herself, gritting her teeth.

"You're not cuttin' off the poor lamb's horn, are you?" demanded Grandmother Bear.

"Certainly not! All I need is a scraping. It's no worse than clipping your claws."

A little curl of unicorn horn dropped into the flask. Phineas shook it vigorously. The flask began to glow.

"Well, here's your cure," said Phineas as Whisper clamped the flask in her teeth. "How you're ever going to get Dorian to take it is beyond me."

With a swish of weary wings, Whisper soared from the hilltop. Squishmire Marsh was overhung with Dorian's smoke. Jets of fire flickered like lightning in storm clouds.

As Whisper approached, the dragon turned a hateful eye upon her. "Begone, insect!" Dorian bellowed. Flames seared the air around her. The tips of her wing feathers curled in the heat. Banking hard, Whisper avoided another blast.

Snap! The last vine parted. Dorian rose on his hind legs, marsh mud oozing from his flanks. Whisper dodged a swat from his claw. All she needed was an opening. She buzzed around Dorian's head like a bee.

"Do you dare attack me! I am Dorian, the new master of Rainbow Forest."

Whisper was exhausted. Each beat of her wings sent an ache through her shoulders. Her head was spinning.

Suddenly the dragon lunged. Whisper felt a blow. She spiraled down, down, landing with a *splat* in the mud. The precious flask plunked on the bank nearby. Dorian hovered, ready to strike.

"Dorian, no! It's me, Whisper. Remember when I used to be afraid to fly? Remember how you told me that all creatures are afraid sometimes? Well, I'm afraid now. I'm afraid for you. Think, Dorian, think who you are. Remember!"

Dorian's horrid expression softened. He tilted his head, looking hard at Whisper.

"Remember…" he hissed. *"Whisper…"*

Just then something sailed through the air. Phineas the Morg had thrown the flask. It struck Dorian on the forehead and burst into a thousand sparkling fragments. Golden light spread down the dragon's long body. It seeped into the marsh water, turning it gold too. Golden mist arose, cleansing the air of smoke and fumes. Dorian sat down in the water and looked curiously at his outstretched claws. Then he glanced at the unicorn in the mud and smiled.

The upper meadows of Rainbow Forest rang with the sound of singing and laughter. A glorious summer picnic was in progress. The guest of honor, Dorian, sat in the midst of his friends. On his right sat Whisper, on his left, Phineas. Never before had there been such a joyous gathering.

"The last time I was here," said Whisper, "I was glad to be alone. Now I'm even gladder we're all together."

"Not half as glad as I am," said Dorian. Grandmother Bear had applied a bandage to the bump on his forehead. He had to look cross-eyed to see it. "I used to pitch for the Nodkin Tigers," Phineas had explained. "My aim's still good. Ha! Ha!"

Bixby jumped up, a mug of carrot juice in his hand. "A toast!" he shouted. "A toast to Dorian, our great friend! And to Whisper, who shows us what friendship means! And to Phineas, the best flask-thrower in Rainbow Forest!"

"Hooray for Dorian!" the crowd shouted. *"Hooray for Phineas! Hooray for Whisper!"*

the
end